abcdefghijklmnopq
ABCDEFGHIJKLMNO
WXYZabcdefghijkl
WXYZABCDEFGHIJ
TUVWXYZabcdef
pqrstuvwxyzABC
MNOPQRSTUVWX
ghijklmnopqrstuv
EFGHIJKLMNLOPQ

FROM ACORN to ZOO

AND EVERYTHING IN BETWEEN IN ALPHABETICAL ORDER

SATOSHI KITAMURA

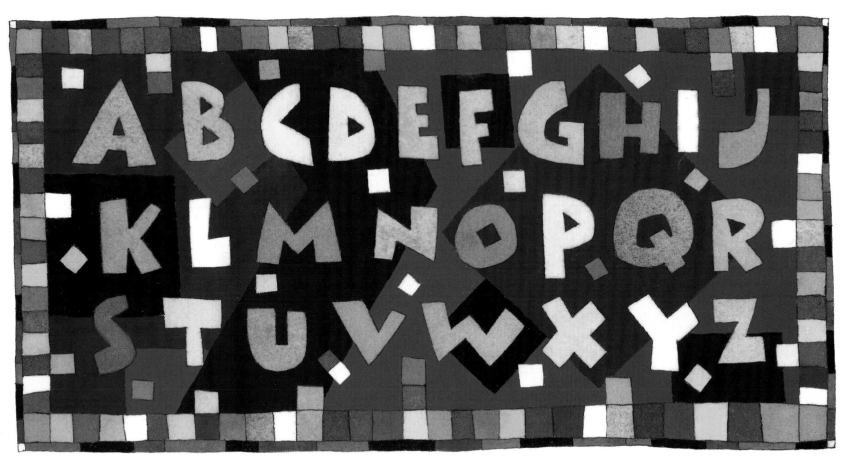

FARRAR, STRAUS AND GIROUX
NEW YORK

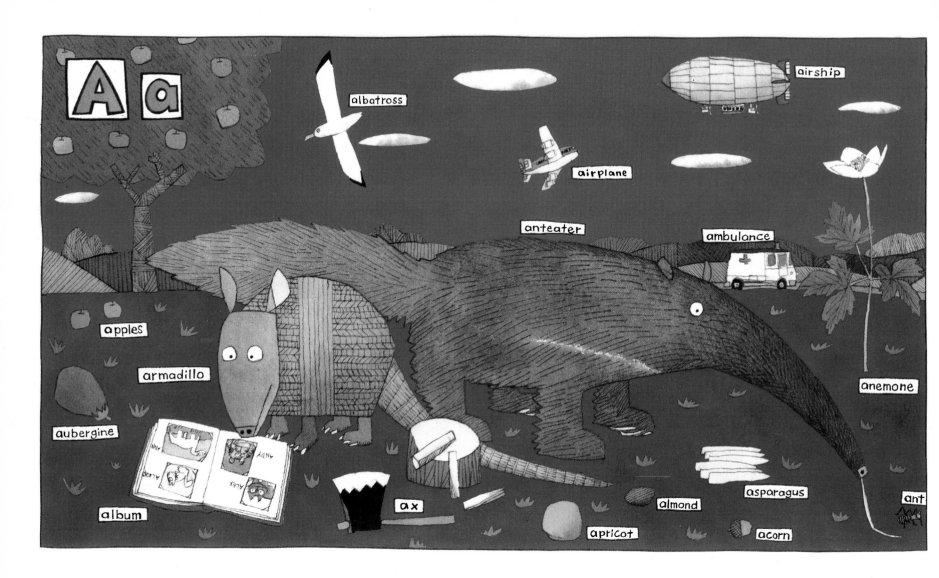

What is the armadillo balancing on his nose?

Bb

brontosaurus
bus
bridge
balloon
bamboo
boat
blackbird
bench
bear
boy
box
book
barrel
bell
bottle
baby
ball
bat
butter
beaver
bag
bicycle
basket
bread
beetle
binoculars

Who's watching Baby go up, up and away?

How does a cat toot a tune to charm a cobra?

D d

dove
daffodil
dolphin
dewdrop
dandelion
dog
daisy
duck
drum
dynamite

Why should Dog
and Duck duck?!

Which came first, the eagle or the…?

With what feathered friend does
Frog share his fruit?

What is the grinning girl holding in her hands?

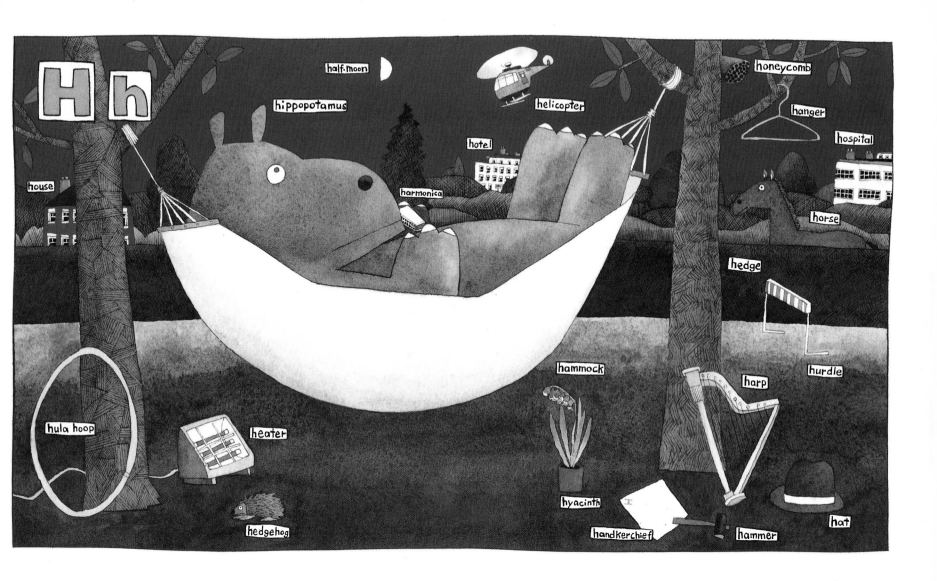

Who's hiding in Hippo's hat?

iceberg

ibis

island

icicle

igloo

ice cream

iron

iris

ivory

iguana

ice

insects

ice skates

ink

How does an eager iguana glide on the ice?

jungle

jet

Jupiter

jewels

jay

jug

juice

jar

jam

PURE ORANGE

STRAWBERRY

jack-in-the-box

jello

jaguar

jelly fish

jigsaw puzzle

What will Jaguar enjoy for dessert?

K k

Kitchen

kite
kingfisher
king
knob
keyhole
koala
kiwi
kangaroo
kettle
knot
knife
knapsack
ketchup
kipper
key
kitten
kennel
kite

"Who's sleeping in the kennel?" caws Kiwi.

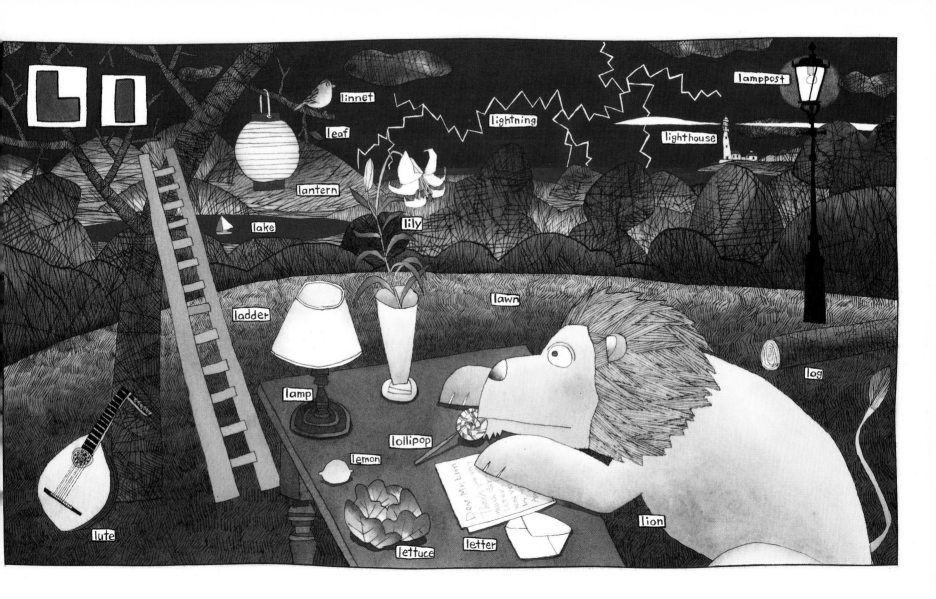

How does Lion light up the night?

"Boo!" says the masked magpie.
Who does he scare?

What does a natty nightingale wear?

Whooo goes out to
sea with Octopus?

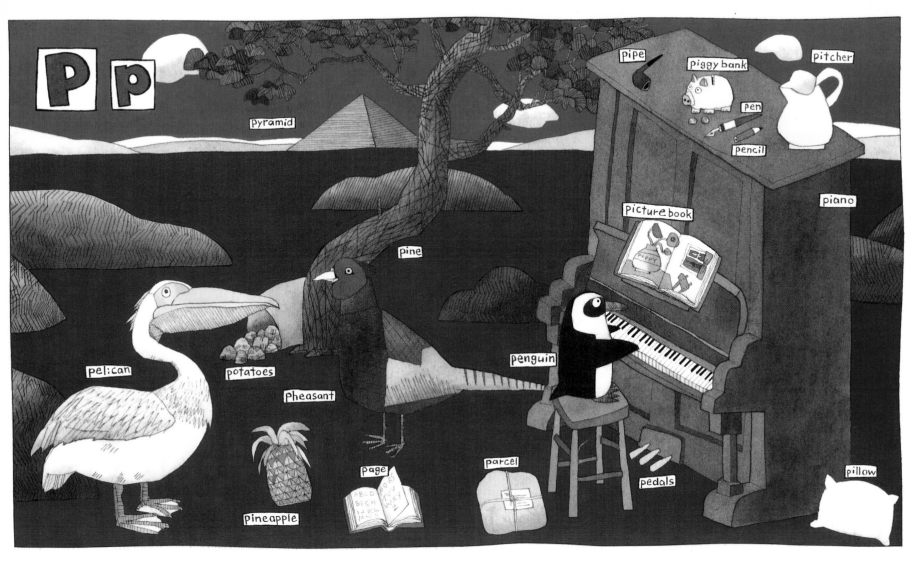

P p

pipe
piggy bank
pitcher
pyramid
pen
pencil
piano
pine
picture book
pelican
potatoes
penguin
Pheasant
page
pineapple
parcel
pedals
pillow

What is Penguin putting
in the postbox?

POST

What can a queen use to make her Q's?

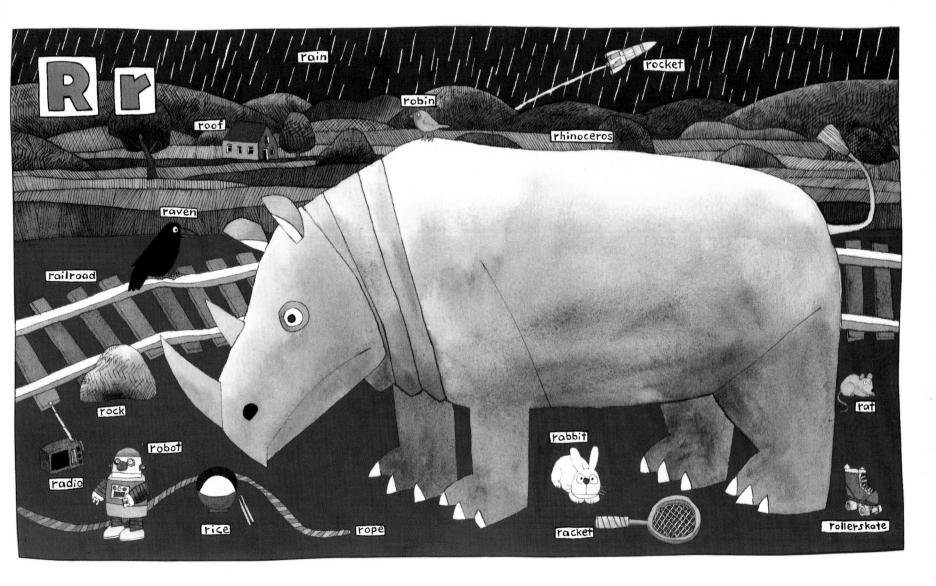

How does Rabbit
race along the road?

S s

sun

Sky

swallow

sea

Submarine

Shoes

Sea gull

socks

snorkel

Sunglasses

Sea horse

Shark

salmon

Sea anemone

Sponge

Sea urchin

Starfish

seaweed

Squid

What should a snazzy sea gull wear
at the seashore?

tower

television

tiger

temple

telescope

tadpoles

telephone

tea

towel

tray

toad

typewriter

table

truck

tiles

tank

turtle

top

taxi

toys

Who watches Turtle while
Turtle watches television?

Up in the sky! What's coming
to visit Unicorn?

volcano

vine

vacuum cleaner

van

vulture

viper

violet

violin

vegetables

vase

Who plays the violin
like a virtuoso?

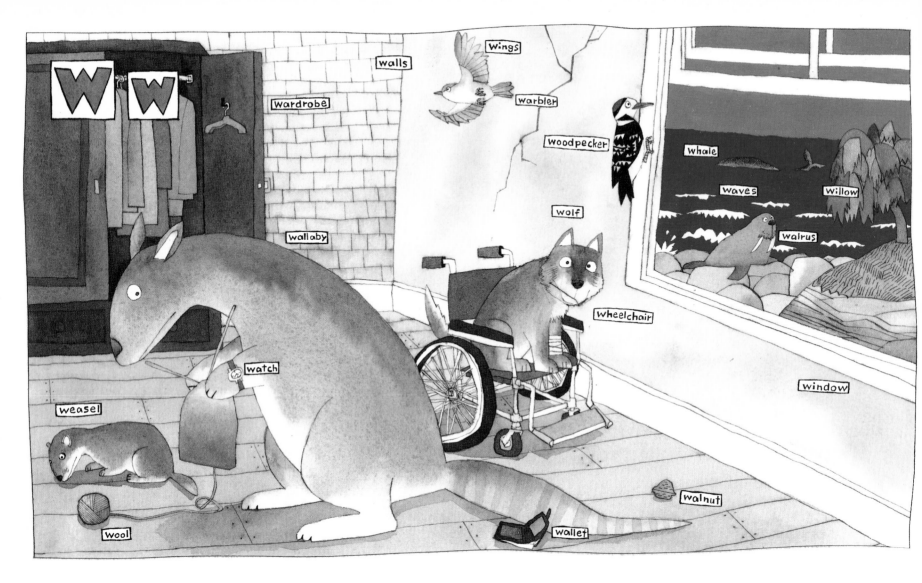

What do Wolf and Wallaby
wear to keep warm?

Yoohoo! Where are Zebra's friends?

abcdefghijklmnopq

ZABCDEFGHIJKLMN

WXYZabcdefghijkl

wxyzABCDEFGHIJ

TUVWXYZabcdef

pqrstuvwxyzABC

MNOPQRSTUVW

ghijklmnopqrstuv

DEFGHIJKLMNOPQ